GODDESSES
A World of Myth and Magic

GODDESSES
A World of Myth and Magic

Written by **Burleigh Mutén**

Illustrated by **Rebecca Guay**

Barefoot Books
Celebrating Art and Story

For every girl who holds this book in her hands — B. M.
For my daughter Vivian — R. G.

Barefoot Books would like to acknowledge the following people, for their help with
the pronunciations of the goddess names: Katherine Griffis-Greenberg, MA;
Professor Tadanori Yamashita; Betsy Mathews and Professor Chün-fang Yü.

We would also like to thank Patricia Monaghan, author of *The New Book of Goddesses
and Heroines* (1997), for her kind help with the fact checking for this book.

Front cover illustration: Aphrodite
Back cover illustration: Zaramama

Barefoot Books
3 Bow Street, 3rd Floor
Cambridge, MA 02138

This book was typeset in Bernhard Modern 12pt on 20pt leading and Kuenstler 165 Bold
The illustrations were prepared in watercolor and acryla-gouache on watercolor paper

Color separation by Grafiscan, Italy
Printed and bound by South China Printing Co. (1988) Ltd.

This book has been printed on 100% acid-free paper

Library of Congress Cataloging-in-Publication Data

Mutén, Burleigh.
Goddesses : a world of myth and magic / retold by Burleigh Mutén ; illustrated by Rebecca Guay.
1st ed. [80] p. : col. ill. ; cm.
Summary: A collection of stories about goddesses from various countries, including information about
where each comes from, her powers, anecdotes and her nature, and details about her sacred animal.
ISBN 1-84148-075-4
1. Goddesses _ Juvenile literature. 2. Mythology _ Juvenile literature. (1. Goddesses. 2. Mythology.) I.
Guay, Rebecca. II. Title.
291.2/114 21 BL473.5.M88 2003
1 3 5 7 9 8 6 4 2

# Introduction

When I was a girl, I was fascinated by the Greek goddess Artemis, Lady of the Wild Things. Not only could she speak with the animals, she lived the exciting life of her dreams in the forest where she ran with the deer. Everyone in the Greek stories knew that Artemis was an accomplished huntress, never missing her mark with her silver bow and arrows. She knew what she wanted and did what she pleased.

I was ten when I first discovered Artemis. Like most girls in the 1950's, I thought sports were for boys. Girls were supposed to be quiet and polite. Artemis was different, and maybe I loved her because I was different myself. How could a girl named Burleigh be anything but different? Maybe I loved Artemis because she defied the authority of her mighty father and insisted on having her own way. What child isn't attracted by independence? I can say this for certain: the stories about Artemis inspired me to think for myself, to believe that I was strong like her, and that I could get what I wanted if I were determined enough.

What I didn't know then was that from the beginning of time, every culture's mythology all over Earth has included powerful goddesses. Not just in Greece, but on every continent on the globe. Some goddesses are so old, there are no written descriptions of what they looked like or what adventures they took part in. The story of Inanna from Sumer is recorded on cuneiform tablets, the oldest known form of writing, which dates back to 2,000 B.C.E.!

Many ancient peoples thought of Earth as female because, like women, the land and sea had the power to generate new life. Stories about a great mother goddess who gave birth to the universe and the first people, plants and animals are found in the mythologies of cultures all over the world. We still call our planet Mother Earth. Oshun from Nigeria, Papatuanuku from New Zealand, and Aditi from India are just a few of the mother goddesses.

But mothering is not the only power goddesses have. Old Feng-Po from China rides through the heavens with a bag containing the wind slung over her shoulder. At her whim, she unties the bag and unleashes breezes as well as big storms. Both Durga and Kali from India are fierce warriors who overthrow demons, while Eirene from Greece proclaims peace on the battlefield. Roman Juno, similar to Hera in Greece, rules over everything that has to do with women — from marriage and pregnancy to childbirth and harmony in the home. Ko-no-Hana from Japan opens the flowering trees each spring. The Greek Muses inspire artists, poets and musicians. Some goddesses shapeshift into animals and some turn themselves into young women when they get old, like Cailleach Beara from Scotland or Estsanatlehi of the Navajo tradition.

Many cultures have never stopped worshiping goddesses. People in India hold celebrations throughout the year to honor numerous goddesses like Lakshmi, goddess of good fortune. The same is true in Mexico and China, as well as many African and South American countries. The strength and power of goddesses continue to inspire women and girls all over the world.

I was a woman and a mother before I realized how many goddesses there are and how many different aspects of life they govern. I wrote this book with the hope that you will discover how adventurous and powerful women deities have been for thousands of years. Maybe you will find one or two or three or four who remind you of yourself!

Burleigh Mutén
Amherst, Massachusetts 2003

A

AATAENTSIC *[EE-yah-tah-HEN-tsik]*
North America / Iroquois

Aataentsic, a creation goddess, married a powerful sorcerer when she was a young maiden. As soon as her husband realized her magic was stronger than his own, he dared Aataentsic to dive through a hole in the sky to get rid of her. Seeing a beautiful world below, Aataentsic raised her arms above her head and dove gracefully through the hole, landing atop a great turtle. Animals of all kinds immediately surrounded the turtle, pushing soil next to its shell. A great island began to take shape, which the Iroquois call Turtle Island. Turtle Island is also called Earth.

ADITI *[ah-DEE-tee]*
India / Hindu

Aditi is called "Mother of the Endless Universe," for she gave birth to the planets, the stars, the sun and moon, the gods and goddesses. She is often represented as a sacred cow, whose milk nourishes everyone and everything on Earth. Children in India still pray to Aditi at night before going to sleep, for Aditi is known for the blessings and protection she bestows upon children.

AMA-TERASU [AH-ma-TAY-rah-soo]
Japan / Shinto

Ama-terasu, goddess of the sun, rules over all the Japanese gods and goddesses, and guards over the Japanese people to this day. Long ago, the gods and goddesses realized how important Ama-terasu was when she retreated into a cave, plunging heaven and Earth into darkness. The desperate deities created a plan. They placed a rooster outside the cave, and when Ama-terasu heard it crow, she wondered how a day could have begun without her. As she peered out of the cave, she saw her own shimmering reflection in a mirror the deities had created. Understanding the importance of her great, brilliant light, Ama-terasu left the cave, never to hide herself again.

APHRODITE [aff-roh-DYE-tee]
Greece

Aphrodite, goddess of love and beauty, was born fully-grown from the foam of the sea. She was exceptionally lovely and enjoyed being admired. She wore a magic girdle that caused everyone who saw her to fall in love with her. But as charming as Aphrodite was in many of the ancient stories, she was also known to be vain and jealous. Today, girls and women continue to worship Aphrodite for her blessings of love, often hoping for romance to enter their lives.
She is similar to the Roman Venus.

A

ARTEMIS *[AHR-tuh-mis]*
Greece

Artemis, goddess of the moon, nature, childbirth and the hunt, still inspires a spirit of confidence and independence in the girls and women who worship her.

At the age of three, Artemis left Mount Olympus, proclaiming that she preferred to reside in the forest with the animals. She asked Zeus, her father, for a bow and arrow, a saffron hunting tunic and a kennel of hunting hounds. Zeus was impressed with her independent spirit, and Artemis set out on her own. In the forest, she studied the healing nature of plants and protected the animals with her silver bow. Because she had helped her mother give birth to her younger brother, Apollo, Greek women often invoked her as they gave birth. The bear and the deer are her sacred animals. Her Roman name is Diana.

ATHENA *[ah-THEE-nah]*
Greece

Athena, goddess of wisdom, was a fierce protectress of the ancient Greeks during times of war, and she still inspires courage in those who worship her. Although Athena is often depicted wearing a plumed helmet and holding a shield, she never carried weapons during peacetime, and she only engaged in battle when the Greeks needed her protection. Athena was a great inventor, credited with creating the arts of weaving, cooking and spinning in addition to the plough, numbers, the flute and the trumpet. Even though many gods wanted to marry Athena, she refused every offer, preferring to be independent. Athena's sacred animal is the owl.

Her Roman name is Minerva.

B

BABD *[Bahv]*
Ireland

Babd, goddess of war, transformed herself into many shapes including the wolf and bear. On the battlefield, Babd appeared in the form of a miniature woman with tiny, webbed feet, screeching of death and doom. The moment the battle ended, Babd quickly changed into the form of a gleaming crow, delighted to feast on the flesh of the dead. Soldiers prayed to Babd, imagining her as a gigantic and beautiful young woman, imploring her to help them cross streams and overcome their enemies. When a soldier saw Babd washing his weapons in a stream, he knew his death was near.

BASTET *[BAHS-tet]*
Egypt

Bastet, goddess of joy, celebration and health, was originally a lion goddess of sunset who ruled over the soft, rosy rays of the afternoon sun. Eventually she was portrayed as a woman with a cat's head. Because domesticated cats protected the grain supply and promoted health by reducing the rodent population, they were Bastet's sacred animals. As part of worshiping her, the ancient Egyptians honored cats. Bastet also inspired wild dancing and lively music. Sunset is her sacred hour.

BEIWE *[BEY-weh]*
Finland

Biewe and her daughter Beiwe-Neida, the sun goddesses, flew through the sky in their chariot of reindeer antlers, shining their bright light through the heavens. Every spring when they arrived after the long, dark months of winter, the people of Finland showed their gratitude by spreading butter on their front doors. As the sun melted the butter, the people believed that the two goddesses were eating it. Together, this mother and daughter blessed the tender green growing plants of spring so the people and the reindeer would have plenty to eat.

BENTEN *[ben-ten]*
Japan / Buddhist

Benten, queen of the sea, is a goddess of good fortune. Every New Year's Eve, she rises from the depths of the sea in the form of a beautiful woman swimming alongside an elaborate treasure ship. The Buddhist people say that if you purchase a picture of the ship and place it under your pillow that night, Benten will reward you with lucky dreams. During the rest of the year, Benten roams the ocean floor in the form of a glorious sea dragon searching for the deep-sea serpents who create earthquakes beneath the Japanese islands. By keeping these rambunctious serpents quiet, Benten maintains peace and prosperity. She also inspires artists with creative ideas and rewards those who are generous with love and wealth.

BRIGIT *[BREED]*
Ireland

Brigit, goddess of fire, healing, poetry and crafts, is one of the oldest known Irish deities. She is still worshiped as a triple goddess, for she appears in three forms — as a young maiden, a nurturing mother, and a wizened crone. As maiden, Brigit inspires Irish poets, musicians, and smiths when they begin their work. As mother, her symbol is the cow with its plentiful milk. As crone, Brigit establishes laws of battle and the safety of women. She invented the whistle so women can be heard at long distances if they are in danger. Brigit was so widely loved by the Irish people, a Christian saint was eventually named after her. Her festival is February 2nd.

BRITOMARTIS *[BRIT-oh-mahr-tis]*
Crete

Britomartis, goddess of the moon, was a clever, active girl who loved to hunt with her bow and arrows. King Minos admired Britomartis, for she was remarkably strong and graceful. He chased her all over the island of Crete, finally cornering her on the edge of a high cliff. Unafraid, Britomartis turned and leaped into the sea. Minos was certain she had died, but Britomartis survived by diving into fishnets that she had invented. Some stories say that she was carried by boat or swam to Greece, where she became known as Artemis. Britomartis was sacred to fishermen, hunters and sailors.

12

B

CAILLEACH BEARA   *[cah-lee-ahk BEAR-ah]*
Scotland, Ireland and England

Cailleach Beara, goddess of the changing seasons, renewed her own youth whenever she was tired of being a hunchbacked, old woman. She had one all-seeing eye in the middle of her deep blue face. Regardless of her age, she was known for her great strength. Some say Cailleach Beara created the great stone structures of Newgrange and Stonehenge by dropping huge boulders from her apron. She also ruled over other aspects of nature, blessing corn crops with abundance and protecting lakes from being drained by blessing the springs beneath them. Cailleach Beara is called the divine ancestor of Scotland. Her sacred animals are the deer and wolf.

CHALCHIUHTLICUE   *[chahl-chew-TLEE-kway]*
Mexico / Aztec

Chalchiuhtlicue, goddess of water, was furious with humans for their wicked ways. She pulled up the oceans and swirled them into a frenzy. Then she directed the rain to pour down from the sky to flood the land. All life was destroyed, except for a few humans and animals who Chalchiuhtlicue transformed into fish. Once the waters subsided, she blessed life on the planet. She continues to bless Earth with rain and is one of the rulers of the night, specifically from 12:33 to 1:38 a.m. Her sacred color is green, and her sacred gem is jade.

CHANG-E [CHAHNG-euh]
China

Chang-E, goddess of the moon, was originally a mortal woman who, by mistake, swallowed a drink of immortality that was intended for her husband. Instantly, Chang-E lifted into the sky, and when she landed on the moon, the hare and the toad who live there welcomed her. The Chinese people still believe that Chang-E looks down to Earth from her home in the sky, protecting children as they sleep. She is also known as Chang-O or Chang-Mu. Her sacred animal is the toad.

CYBELE [SIH-beh-lee]
Greece, Turkey and Italy

Cybele, one of the oldest known creation goddesses, blessed the crops every spring with abundance. The ancient peoples believed that the spirit of Cybele resided in a great, black meteorite, which landed on Earth more than 3,000 years ago. In 204 B.C.E., this sacred stone was laboriously moved from Turkey to Italy in a ship made of wood from Cybele's sacred fir trees. The rock was then loaded onto a grand chariot, which carried it across land to Cybele's temple in Rome. For several centuries, Romans adorned statues of Cybele with roses on her festival day, April 4th. The lion is her sacred animal.

D

DEMETER *[dih-MEE-tur or DEH-meh-tur]*
Greece

Gentle Demeter, goddess of grain, blessed the crops each spring so they would grow. Girls and women still worship Demeter as a loyal mother, for she was fiercely devoted to her daughter, Persephone. When Hades, ruler of the underworld, kidnapped Persephone and took her to his underworld kingdom, Demeter was so grief-stricken and furious, she refused to bless the crops until Persephone was returned to her side. For over 2,000 years, the Greeks celebrated Demeter and Persephone in a religious ritual known as the Thesmorphoria. The sheath of wheat, the poppy and the pig are Demeter's sacred symbols. Her Roman name is Ceres.

DURGA *[DOOR-gah]*
India / Hindu

Durga, a fierce warrior, was born during a lengthy battle between the Hindu gods and an army of demons. In desperation, the gods gathered together and breathed in unison. A ferocious fire blazed forth from their mouths, out of which Durga was born — a fully-grown warrior, ready to fight. The gods quickly gave her a lion to mount and a weapon for each of her ten hands. Durga advanced toward the demons, her arms flashing, and within moments she had slaughtered them all. To the Indian people, Durga symbolizes triumph over evil. They still celebrate her for nine days every fall.

D

E

ECHO *[EH-koh]*
Greece

Echo, a mountain nymph, loved rhyming, chanting and telling long, entertaining stories. Once, when Echo tried to trick Queen Hera by distracting her with idle chatter, Hera punished Echo by taking away her voice. Thereafter, Echo was only able to repeat the last syllable of each word she heard. To this day, Echo's spirit remains in mountain valleys, gorges and caves, repeating the last syllable of whatever she hears.

EIRENE *[eye-REEN-ee]*
Greece

Eirene, goddess of peace, became impatient because there were so many battles in ancient Greece. She retreated to the mountains with her sisters, the Horae (Dike, whose name means justice, and Eunomia, whose name means order). Whenever a war ended, Eirene came down from the mountain to proclaim peace on the battlefield. She was often seen burying or burning weapons. Her Roman name is Pax.

ELLI *[EH-lee]*
Scandinavia

Elli, goddess of old age, was so strong that no one could defeat her. Refusing to believe she was invincible, Thor, the powerful thunder god, challenged her to a wrestling match he was sure he would win. He laughed when he saw how frail and weak Elli appeared to be, but the moment the match began, Thor realized his error in judgment. Elli had no trouble overpowering him, for no one can defeat old age.

EPONA *[eh-POH-nah]*
France, England, Italy

Epona, a beautiful half-horse, half-woman, brought good fortune to horses and horsemen. She was the child of a mare and a mortal king, which gave her the ability to take either form — human or horse. She was especially popular with cavalry soldiers, who sought her protection. Statues of Epona as a horse-headed woman, as a mare suckling her foal and as a woman riding a horse, were kept in stables as well as in soldiers' saddlebags. She was often portrayed carrying a cornucopia or a key, or accompanied by a raven, which are symbols of bounty and blessing. Originally Celtic, Epona's worship spread throughout Europe into Africa.

ESTSANATLEHI *[es-tan-AHT-luh-hee]*
North America / Navajo

Estsanatlehi, goddess of time, magic, life, death and immortality, lives in a turquoise palace in the sky, which is why she is sometimes called Turquoise Woman. Whenever Estsanatlehi begins to age, she walks toward the east until she finds her young self walking toward her. Estsanatlehi is still invoked by the Navajo people during sacred ceremonies to bless young girls coming into their womanhood. She is also known as Changing Woman and is considered to be the mother of the four great Navajo clans.

ETERNA [ee-TER-nah]
China

Eterna, goddess of sorcery, was especially gifted in the arts of transformation and the multiplication of wealth. As an infant, Eterna was swept into the air by a forceful black wind, separating her from her mother. By the time Eterna's mother found her, Eterna had already been reborn into a family of merchants. For years, Eterna's mother made secret visits to the child, teaching her the art of sorcery. Using this magic, Eterna saved her new family from starvation by multiplying the few coins they had left. Her father was so horrified by Eterna's magical power, he attempted to kill her! Eterna's mother interceded and finally brought Eterna to her underworld home, where they still reside in a jeweled palace rimmed with enormous, ancient trees.

EURYNOME [yoo-RIH-nuh-mee]
Greece

Eurynome, the Mother of All Things, danced along the waves of the vast, dark sea in the time before the beginning of time. She sensed someone behind her and turned to find Ophion, the great serpent, with whom she mated. Eurynome then turned herself into a dove and laid an enormous egg. Ophion coiled himself around the egg until it cracked open, giving birth to all things that exist: the sun, moon, planets, stars, mountains, rivers, trees and all living creatures including the gods and goddesses. Eurynome is the grandmother of Zeus.

F

THE FATIT *[FAH-tit]*
Albania

The Fatit, goddesses of fate, took the form of three miniature women. Three days after a child was born, the Fatit flew into the baby's room on the backs of butterflies. As they approached the cradle, they began to sing. Hovering over the baby, each goddess foretold a portion of the child's life story from that day forth to the day of its death.

FENG-PO *[FEHNG-poh]*
China

Old Feng-Po, mistress of wind, rides a great tiger through the heavens with a big, billowing bag slung over her shoulder. When she is ready, she loosens the cord on her bag and releases the wind, commanding it to swirl toward the east or sweep slowly southward. She delights as she hears the leaves rustling in the trees. She laughs as she listens to thunder or the low, roaring howl of a hurricane. When the heavens are calm, we know Feng-Po has stuffed the wind back into her bag.

FORTUNA *[fohr-TOO-nah]*
Italy

Fortuna, goddess of fortune, blessed humans with good luck and the Earth with abundance. A blind goddess, Fortuna made decisions based on her intuition, not by what she could see. The ancient Romans created statues of Fortuna holding the rudder of a boat and a cornucopia full of fruit — symbolizing both the journey she steered for humans as well as the abundance she provided to nourish the planet. Her Greek name is Tyche.

FREYA *[FRAY-ah]*
Scandinavia

Freya, goddess of love, magic, death and war, was a beautiful and powerful sorceress, who hovered over every battlefield in her golden chariot drawn by two cats, waiting for the battle to end. As soon as the last soldier died, Freya swept down to Earth to select those lucky dead soldiers who would thereafter reside in her castle, feasting and celebrating for eternity. Freya blessed the harvests with abundance and took special care of women who were preparing to marry or give birth. She taught magic to all the northern gods, but she let no one wear her falcon cloak that gave her the power to soar swiftly from heaven to Earth. The boar is her sacred animal.

GAIA *[JEE-uh]*
Greece

Gaia, one of the oldest creation goddesses, is still known as Mother Earth. The ancient Greeks worshiped and prayed to Gaia in mountain caves and in groves of the oldest trees. Eventually, they built temples in her honor at Delphi on the side of gleaming, white Mount Parnassas, where it was believed that Gaia spoke to mortals through her priestesses. For over 3,000 years, kings and politicians, poets and parents sought Gaia's guidance and wisdom at Delphi. Many people concerned with ecology and the health of our planet still worship Gaia.

Her sacred animal is the serpent, and her Roman name is Tellus.

GENDENWITHA *[gen-den-WITH-uh]*
North America / Iroquois

Gendenwitha, goddess of the morning star, was originally a mortal woman who loved to dance beneath the star-filled sky. One night as she danced, Great Night, the doorkeeper for Dawn, fell in love with Gendenwitha. Dawn, goddess of the new day, was jealous, so she turned Gendenwitha into a star that she placed on her own forehead. Immortalized by Dawn, Gendenwitha became the morning star, the first bright star to shine as the sun rises.

G

GOGA *[GOH-gah]*
New Guinea

Goga, goddess of fire, was old but no matter how old she became, she renewed her strength and immortality with a magical fire that glowed within her body. Her ageless nature was a mystery to everyone, until a boy who was spying on Goga saw her pull the blazing flames out of herself. Thrilled and excited, the bold boy stuck a branch into the fire and ran for his life. Goga called to the heavens for rain to quell the fire. The boy jumped into a hollow tree, which ignited and attracted the attention of the villagers nearby. Realizing she had lost her secret power, Goga taught the people of New Guinea how to use fire in many ways, including sacred ceremony.

THE GRACES
Greece

The Graces, goddesses of beauty, joy and kindness, were the beautiful sisters named Thalea (She Who Opens All the Flowers), Euphrosyne (She Who Makes Glad) and Aglai (Shining One). They inspired the ancient Greeks with good manners and the delight that comes from art, music and dance. Wherever they went, they created joy, increasing the happiness of all who saw them. The Graces inspired artists and poets with creative ideas. At any important occasion, the host would pour the first cup of wine in honor of the Graces to ensure that a good time would be had by all present.

THE GRAEAE *[GRY-eye* or *GREE-ee]*
Greece

Pemphredo, Enyo and Deino were white-haired, old women when they were born, which is why they were called the Old Ones. As they grew older, they continued to age, becoming more and more feeble until they had only one tooth and one eye, which they shared among themselves. Since the Graeae were responsible for guarding their sisters — Medusa and the Gorgons — they used their intuition and keen hearing to sense approaching danger. They often transformed themselves into swans, their sacred bird.

HANNA HANNA   *[HAN-nah HAN-nah]*
Near East, Anatolia / Hittite

Ancient Hanna Hanna, goddess of wisdom, foretold the future and was called upon in times of trouble. Once, when the water god Telipinu fell into a deep sleep, no one could find him. Wells, rivers and streams dried up. Crops withered. In desperation, everyone prayed to Hanna Hanna, who immediately dispatched her sacred bee to find the sleeping god. When the bee startled him awake with a sharp sting, Telipinu was furious and confused. Hanna Hanna's sacred eagle soared down from the sky, insisting that Telipinu climb onto its back, and carried him quickly to Hanna Hanna. She told him about the drought, and Telipinu quickly blessed the land with rain.

HATHOR   *[HAH-thor]*
Egypt

Hathor, goddess of light, was loved and worshiped by the ancient Egyptians for over 3,000 years. They referred to her as the Gentle Cow of Heaven for her plentiful milk, which nourished not only her son, Ra, the sun god, but all life as well. She nursed the infant pharaohs, making each of them divine. Hathor was also called Lady of the Sycamore, the sacred tree on the edge of the underworld, because she waited beneath its ancient branches to greet and guide the dead. Hathor also took the form of the rattle, an instrument used in festival dancing. She brought happiness to all celebrations.

H

HEKATE *[hek-AH-tay* or *HEK-ah-tee]*
Greece

Hekate, queen of the night, the moon and magic, was a powerful sorceress. On the night of the new moon, the ancient Greeks placed plates of food for old Hekate at the intersections of three roads, her sacred ground. Some ancient poets described her as an old woman accompanied by three dogs, and some described her as having three heads herself — that of a horse, a serpent and a dog. In exchange for the offerings left for her, Hekate bestowed upon mortals the gifts of wealth, wisdom and victory. The ancient Greeks placed small statues of Hekate next to the doors of their homes to prevent evil from entering. Her sacred symbols are the key, the dagger and the rope.

HEL *[HEL]*
Scandinavia

Hel, goddess of the underworld, rode a black horse through the dark every night, calling the names of those who would die of old age or disease before dawn. As spirits left the bodies of the dead, Hel wrapped her old arms around them and lifted them into her cart. She traveled far and wide with her cartful of spirits, always managing to reach the entrance to the Troublesome Road on the edge of the underworld just before dawn. Hel's palace, which she called Sleet Cold, was made of human bones, worms and decaying wood.

HERA *[HEER-ah or HAIR-ah]*
Greece

Hera, goddess of the sky, watched over, protected and guided women as they prepared to marry, conceive children and give birth. When Hera married Zeus, Mother Earth gave her a tree with golden apples, the blessing of immortality. Thereafter, Hera was known for her magnificent garden of eternal life. She was also known as a great leader, who had the power to ease childbirth and to foretell the future. The original athletic games, which were played in a stadium adjacent to Hera's temple in Olympia, were dedicated to Hera. Only women were allowed to compete. Hera is similar to the Roman goddess Juno. The peacock is her sacred bird.

HESTIA *[HES-tee-ah]*
Greece

Hestia, goddess of domestic life, was one of the most revered goddesses in the Olympian pantheon, for she ruled over the flame that burned in each household's hearth. Hestia, who was tall and stately, refused to allow any harsh words or disagreement in her temple. Girls and women often invoked Hestia, asking for her blessings of peace, harmony and happiness within the family. Whenever a Greek village's public hearth was extinguished for any reason, a runner was sent to Hestia's temple where her perpetual flame burned night and day. Hestia never married. She is similar to the Roman goddess Vesta.

IDUNA *[ee-DOO-nah]*
Scandinavia

Iduna, goddess of youth, tended her orchard with care, for the gods and goddesses depended on her apples to keep them young and full of energy. Once, when Iduna was captured by a group of giants, the Norse gods and goddesses quickly began to weaken and wither with age. As soon as Iduna was rescued, she fed the frightened, decrepit deities her potent apples, and they were quickly restored to their vibrant, youthful selves. Iduna also invented the runes — small stones inscribed with magical symbols that are used for seeing the future.

INANNA *[ee-NAN-nah]*
Mesopotamia / Sumer

Inanna, goddess of love and war, was worshiped by the ancient Sumerians for over 3,000 years. As a warrior goddess, she was a powerful leader who inspired her soldiers to fight fiercely. As a goddess of love, she blessed the land each spring with plentiful rain. Inanna believed that she could do anything, and she decided to embark on a perilous journey — to visit the underworld, a place from which no one had ever returned. Her sister, Erishkegal, who was the queen of the dead, stripped Inanna of her jewels and killed her. After three days, Inanna's faithful servant revived her, and Inanna resumed her position as queen of Heaven. The ancient Sumerians worshiped the morning and evening stars, the first to shine brightly at dawn and dusk, as forms of Inanna.

I

I

IRIS [EER-is or EYE-ris]
Greece

Iris, goddess of the rainbow, was the good-natured and faithful servant of Queen Hera. Always ready for her mistress's next request, Iris stood patiently beside Hera's throne. When dispatched, she flung open her golden wings and rose into the air, leaving a rainbow trailing behind her. Whenever the gods or goddesses proclaimed a solemn oath, Iris soared through the sky and the sea to the underworld, where she fetched a cup of water from the River Styx. As the gods spoke their promises, Iris slowly poured the water from the cup as a gesture to ensure the oath's truth. Her rainbow eventually became a symbol of hope.

ISIS *[EYE-sis or EE-sis]*
Egypt

Isis, the great healer, was worshiped by the ancient Egyptians for over 7,000 years. She knew the healing powers of plants and created the first pharmacy of medicinal plants, which she used to heal her own son, Horus, who was weak and sickly at birth. Isis taught women how to heal with plants and how to weave and spin cloth. Isis was also a powerful enchantress who shape-shifted into many animal forms including birds and fish. Because she ruled over so many aspects of life, Isis was referred to by many different names and was eventually called "Lady of Ten Thousand Names."

IX CHEL *[EESH CHEL]*
Mexico / Maya, Putun

Ix Chel, goddess of the moon, bestows blessings of fertility upon women who worship her. She is also honored as a great teacher who showed women how to weave cloth, an art that she learned by watching a spider weave its web. When Ix Chel was young, she ran away with her lover, the sun. Her possessive, old grandfather threw a lightning bolt at her, killing her instantly. Hundreds of dragonflies swarmed over Ix Chel's body for thirteen days and nights, bringing her back to life. She eagerly reunited with the sun, but soon realized that she preferred her independence. One night she took the form of a great sphere of white light, silently rising into the sky, where she has roamed ever since, disappearing once a month whenever the sun gets too close to her.

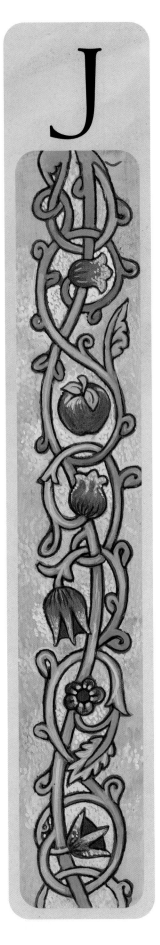

JUNKGOWA SISTERS *[junk-GOW-ah]*
Australia / Yulengor

The Junkgowa Sisters, ancient goddesses of creation, made the sea, and then constructed a canoe to explore the world. The sisters sang as they paddled, creating fish, sea plants and mammals with their magical words, until they reached the shore. Full of excitement and curiosity, they walked from one place to the next, striking their walking sticks on the ground, creating sacred waterholes that connected to the spirit world. The Junkgowa Sisters gave birth to the first people. They created fire as well as numerous sacred and practical objects for their children. Unfortunately, when their sons reached adulthood, they stole the Junkgowa Sisters' ceremonial objects, and the sisters disappeared into the sea.

JUNO *[JOO-noh]*
Italy

Juno, the supreme goddess of the ancient Romans, ruled over everything that had to do with women. She made sure that weddings were properly prepared. She walked alongside the bride on her way to the groom's home, and she watched to make sure he carried the bride over the threshold.

Juno protected pregnant women, helped them as they gave birth, and strengthened the bones of newborn babies. Women who were barren prayed to Juno for children. Every year, on the 7th of March, the women of Rome honored Juno with a great celebration called the Matronalia. Geese and peacocks are sacred to Juno. She is similar to the Greek goddess, Hera.

K

KAGUYA-HIME *[KA-goo-YAH-hee-may]*
Japan / Shinto

Kaguya-hime, lovely goddess of the moon, once traveled to Earth in the form of a glowing, miniature woman. An old woodcutter in the forest was startled when he heard a beautiful song coming from the roots of a bamboo shoot and discovered Kaguya-hime hiding there. The woodcutter and his wife adopted the miniature woman, and from that day forth, their fortune increased. Word of the wondrous singing woman spread until even the emperor desired to court her. Kaguya-hime began to yearn for her home in the city on the moon, and when the emperor heard this news, he collapsed in distress. Before she returned to the moon, Kaguya-hime blessed the loving emperor with the gift of eternal youth.

KALI *[KAH-lee]*
India / Hindu

Kali, the great mother, gives life, and she destroys it. To the Hindu people, Kali is both a fierce warrior and a loyal, protective mother who cures disease and calms the fears of those who worship her. Once, after decapitating a huge, hideous demon, Kali was astonished to see the monster's blood turning into thousands of giants. Realizing she had no choice, Kali lapped up the blood of the demon. Thrilled with her success and somewhat crazed by what she had just done, Kali launched into a wild and frenzied dance, her long hair swirling around her as she stamped her feet and flailed her arms. Within moments, the earth was quaking, and the gods had to intercede to calm Kali down. Many Indian people still hang Kali's picture in their homes to help them conquer their worst fears.

K

K

KO-NO-HANA [KOH-noh-HAN-nah]
Japan / Shinto

Ko-no-Hana, goddess of the flowering trees, was cursed by her jealous sister, the mistress of long life. Thereafter, Ko-no-Hana's sacred tree, the cherry tree, had an exceptionally short blossoming season. When Ko-no-Hana married and became pregnant, her foolish husband doubted whether the unborn child was actually his. Ko-no-Hana gave birth to three healthy babies and placed them into a fire, proclaiming that any child of hers who had not been fathered by her husband would perish in the fire.

All three babies survived.

KORRIGAN [KOHR-ih-gan]
France

Korrigan, goddess of underground springs, was the granddaughter of a
powerful druid queen. She lived beneath sacred temples and appeared at
night as a beautiful, translucent, miniature maiden. During the day, when
Korrigan mingled with mortals, she took the form of a withered old woman.
Protective of women and of her own privacy, Korrigan was quick to kill or
kidnap any man who spied on her secret rituals or brought harm to a woman.
Today Korrigan is thought of as a fairy.

KUAN YIN [KWAN YIN or GWAN YIN]
China / Buddhist

Kuan Yin, who bestows mercy and kindness, is one of China's most popular
goddesses and is worshiped all over the world. She was originally a mortal
princess named Maio Shan, who preferred praying and helping stray animals
to participating in the traditions of her regal family. Maio Shan's father
disapproved of her spiritual life and ordered his soldiers to kill her. After her
death, the Great Mother Goddess, Xi Wang Mu, blessed Maio Shan for her
goodness by giving her immortality and a new name, Kuan Yin, which means
She Who Hears the Cries of the World. People still believe she looks down
to Earth, always ready to help those who remember to call her name.

L

LAKSHMI *[LAKSH-mee]*
India / Hindu

Lakshmi, goddess of prosperity, blesses mortals with abundance and good fortune. She was born from the churning sea, a fully-grown woman adorned with jewels and pearls, holding a lotus in her hand. Many gods wanted to marry Lakshmi for her remarkable beauty and her exceptional kindness, but she chose Vishnu, the loving sun god, as her husband for many lifetimes. In order to win the favor of Lakshmi, Hindus place small pots of holy basil, which is sacred to her, near their dwellings and temples. On the night of the new moon every November, women place candles and lanterns outside their homes to attract Lakshmi's attention.

LIA *[LEE-ah]*
Australia / Goanna

Lia, goddess of water and guardian of women, looked down from the sky and noticed a group of people in the dry, dusty desert. She saw that the men, who left every day in search of water, were clean while the women, who dug for roots all day, were thirsty and covered with dust. One day while the men were gone, Lia led the women into the mountains to look for their own water. She found the right spot and struck her walking stick on the ground, opening a rushing stream that quickly widened into a flowing river. When the men returned that night, they saw the women laughing and clean on the other side of the river, where they had created their own village with Lia as their leader.

LILITH *[LIH-leth]*

Mesopotamia / Sumer

Lilith, goddess of wisdom, was fiercely independent and strong-willed — she didn't care what anyone thought of her choices. When her husband tried to tell Lilith what she could and couldn't do, she spread her wings, rose into the sky, and flew away, refusing to return. Lilith gave birth to many children and raised them by herself, later becoming a protectress of newborn babies during their first week of life. She was also considered a goddess of the night winds, who conjured storms of all kinds.

MACHA *[MAH-kah]*
Ireland

Macha, goddess of war, was a mighty queen of the Celtic people.
She was so powerful that when two neighboring kings objected to a
woman ruler, Macha assembled an army and defeated both kings and
their armies. She was so beautiful, many opposing soldiers gawked at her,
rendering them helpless, easy prey. Macha's husband, who loved to boast
about her strength, grace and speed, once made a wager that she could
run faster than horses. Since Macha was pregnant, she asked for the race
to be delayed, but her husband insisted she run. Macha easily strode
ahead of the horses, won the race, and collapsed as she gave birth to
twins. Panting with exhaustion and humiliated by giving birth in public,
Macha cursed all the men present, as well as their male descendants for
nine generations. Subsequently, these men would feel the pain of
childbirth for five days and nights so they would never forget
what a woman experiences when she gives birth.

MAMA PACCHA *[MAH-mah PAH-chah]*
Peru / Inca

Mama Paccha, a creation goddess, made the mountains and taught
women how to plant and harvest corn. She then took the shape of a
glorious dragon, which is said to reside deep within the Andes Mountains.
The people of Peru still make daily prayers to Mama Paccha, their Dragon
Mother, so she will not rub herself against the inner walls of the mountains,
creating earthquakes. And to this day, women talk and sing to Mama
Paccha as they work in their gardens and in the fields.

M

MBABA MWANA WARESA
[mm-BAH-bah mm-WAN-ah wah-REH-sah] South Africa / Zulu

Mbaba Mwana Waresa, a rain goddess who governs storm clouds, lightning and thunder, fell in love with a mortal man. In order to make sure he loved her, Mbaba Mwana Waresa tested her beloved by sending a beautiful bride in her place, while she disguised herself as an ugly hag. Her earthly lover wasn't fooled. He recognized Mbaba Mwana Waresa immediately. They married, and to this day live together in her rainbow-covered house in the sky. The Zulu still call on Mbaba Mwana Waresa when they want guidance to make important decisions.

MEDUSA *[meh-DOO-sah]*
Greece

Medusa was the youngest and only mortal of the three Gorgon sisters who lived in the depths of the far western sea. Beautiful Medusa was renowned for her gleaming, gold wings and her long, golden hair that twirled into serpentine ringlets. Many heroes feared Medusa and considered her a monster because of her fatal gaze, which could turn men to stone. When the Greek hero Perseus killed Medusa, she immediately gave birth to Pegasus, the winged horse, who flew out of her body into the sky. After she died, Medusa's blood was used to revive the dead.

THE MUSES
Greece

The Muses, goddesses of creativity, still inspire poets, dancers, painters, sculptors, astronomers and playwrights all over the world. The nine Muses were sisters, each of whom was said to govern a particular art or science. Calliope, whose name means Beautiful Voice, is goddess of narrative poetry. Clio, whose name means Fame Giver, carries an open scroll in which she takes note of all those she blesses. Euterpe, whose name means Giver of Joy, plays the flute and is goddess of lyric poetry. Thalia, whose name means Festive One, carries the comic mask and is goddess of comedy. Melpomene, whose name means Sorrowful One, carries the tragic mask and is goddess of tragedy. Terpsicore, whose name means Lover of Dancing, carries a lyre and is goddess of dance. Erato, whose name means Awakening of Desire, also carries a lyre and is goddess of sensual poetry. Polyhymnia, whose name means Many Hymns, is goddess of sacred song. And Urania, whose name means Heavenly, holds a globe of the stars and planets and is the goddess of astronomy.

The Muses were gifted musicians and whenever they sang, whether it was in the forest or at a gathering of the gods and goddesses, all who heard their chorus were spellbound by the beauty of their voices. They were also gifted in the art of foretelling the future.

N

NGOLIMENTO [nn-gol-ee-men-toh]
Togo / Ewe

Ngolimento, mother of spirits, is still worshiped by the Togo people as the goddess who cares for the spirits of children before they are born. If unborn children obey Ngolimento, they will enjoy an easy birth and a happy life on Earth. If they do not cooperate with their spirit mother, she curses them with a difficult birth, bad health or a series of misfortunes in their earthly life.

NIKE [NYE-kee]
Greece

Nike, whose name means Victory, was a winged maiden, who, along with her sisters, Zeal, Power and Force, helped Zeus to win the battle against his forefathers, the Titans. Mortals prayed for Nike's protection during times of war or whenever they began dangerous journeys. The wreath of bay leaves Nike wore on her head is still used today as a symbol of success. Her Roman name is Victoria.

NINLIL *[nin-lil]*
Babylonia, Sumer

Ninlil, mistress of winds and mother of the moon, was worshiped by the
ancient Sumerians. She lived in the underworld with her husband, the king
of the dead. After she became pregnant, Ninlil dreamed her unborn child
was the moon. Realizing that her son would not be able to reach the sky
from beneath Earth's surface, Ninlil created a plan. Just before she gave
birth, Ninlil told her husband she needed some fresh air. As she strolled
along under the stars, her son emerged from her womb, and Ninlil conjured
a swift, gentle wind to lift the boy carefully into the sky. Ninlil's symbols
are the serpent and the tree with entwined branches.

49

NORWAN *[NOR-wahn]*
North America / Wintun

Norwan is called "Dancing Porcupine Woman," for she never stops dancing from dawn to dusk. A child of Mother Earth and the sun, Norwan nourishes edible, green growing plants by dancing above them in the form of a wisp of warm light. Her sacred animal is the porcupine.

NÜ WA *[NU WAH]*
China

Nü Wa, the ancient Chinese goddess of creation and marriage, has the head of a beautiful woman and the body of a giant serpent. In the beginning of time, right after she made the mountains and trees, Nü Wa sculpted a miniature clay statue of herself. When she placed the tiny figure on Earth's soil, the little woman began to move, calling Nü Wa "Mother." Nü Wa smiled and quickly made many more miniature humans. Realizing that they were mortal, she made an equal amount of males and females, so they could create more of their own kind. Nü Wa was also a goddess of matchmaking, bringing men and women together so they would fall in love. The snail is her sacred animal.

OBA *[o-BAH]*
Nigeria / Yoruba

Oba, goddess of the river, is still worshiped by the Yoruba people as a nurturing mother, who gives them water for drinking and bathing, for use in sacred ceremony, and for crops. Once long ago, Oba tricked her sister, Oya, into believing that the handsome god of thunder treasured the delicacy of cooked ear! Eager to please him, Oba's gullible sister cut off her own ear and served it to the god. He was disgusted and turned away. To this day in Nigeria, the waters of the Oba and Oya rivers are always turbulent where they intersect.

OLWEN *[OHL-wen]*
Wales

Olwen, goddess of sunlight, appeared only in springtime and summer. Wherever she went, she left a trail of white clover behind her. Every spring, she opened the blossoms of all flowering trees and plants. Olwen's father loved her dearly, perhaps too dearly. When she told him she intended to marry her own true love, the old man insisted she accomplish thirteen impossible tasks before she could marry. To his dismay, clever Olwen mastered all of the tasks and married her true love.

OPS *[OPS]*
Italy

Ops, goddess of agriculture, lived in a cave deep within the Earth and taught women how and when to plant seeds, as well as how and when to harvest crops. Many Roman women prayed to Ops for abundance, since their very existence depended on the food they grew. Whether a woman was praying for plentiful food or for the health of her child, she would bend down and touch the ground with her hand as a form of prayer to Ops. Great banquets honoring Ops were served on August 25th as part of the harvest. Slaves were served by their masters, schools and courts of law were closed and wars were delayed. People gave gifts of wax candles to each other.

OSHUN *[oh-SHOON]*
Nigeria / Yoruba and Brazil, Cuba and Haiti

Oshun, goddess of creation, is considered to be the mother of the Yoruba people. Women still pray to Oshun when they want to have children. She protects women leaders and cures the sick with water from the river that bears her name. Oshun gave birth to the first people on Earth with such ease, all the gods in heaven were impressed. Oshun is also worshiped in Brazil, Cuba and Haiti, where she represents wealth and prosperity.
Her symbols are the brass bracelet and the pumpkin.

OSTARA *[oh-STAR-ah]*
Germany

Ostara is the goddess of spring. Her festival eventually became known as Eastre, a festival of joyous parades and bell-ringing in honor of the increasing sunlight in spring that nourishes bountiful crops. Rabbits and painted eggs were also used in this celebration to symbolize abundance. Some scholars say that Easter grew out of this traditional celebration of the turning of seasons.

PANDORA *[pan-DOHR-ah]*
Greece

Beautiful Pandora is best known for her curiosity and the box she opened, which released all forms of evil into the world, including sickness, death and war. Realizing what she'd done, Pandora slammed the lid shut just in time to prevent hope from escaping. Some scholars say that her real name was Pandora Gaia and that she was originally the all-giving Earth Mother herself.

PAPATUANUKU *[pah-pah-too-ah-noo-koo]*
New Zealand / Maori

Papatuanuku, Mother Earth, mated with Rango, the sky, and gave birth to the sun and moon. She then gave birth to animals, plants, birds and insects of all kinds. Her sons, who were gods, immediately got to work creating order among the new life-forms while Papatuanuku stared up at Rango, who was and still is gazing down at her.

PELE *[PAY-lay]*
Polynesia / Hawaii

Pele, goddess of volcanic fire and mother of the Hawaiian islands, was fascinated with fire from the time she was a child. Once, as she argued with her sister, Namak, who was a water goddess, the two sisters struggled until Namak killed Pele. Pele's spirit fled into a volcano, which spewed forth fiery eruptions, creating the Hawaiian islands. To this day, it is said that when Pele is angry, she appears as an old woman or as a young girl on the rim of a volcano, stamping her foot to start an eruption.

PERSEPHONE *[per-SEH-foh-nee]*
Greece

Beautiful, young Persephone, queen of the dead, resided in the underworld for six months of the year. Her absence from Earth's surface created winter. When she returned to Earth's surface in spring, Persephone and her mother, Demeter, blessed the crops and opened all the leaves and flowers. After the fall harvest, gentle Persephone once again returned to the underworld to guide the dead until the following spring. Today, girls and women invoke Persephone in springtime as a symbol of new beginnings.

QADESH *[kah-desh]*

Egypt

Qadesh, called the "Holy One," is the Egyptian goddess of love, sensuality and fertility. She is most commonly depicted riding on the back of a lion, sometimes standing up, holding out snakes, lotus buds or papyrus plants — all of which are symbols of fertility. Quadesh was also worshiped by the Egyptians as a goddess of nature.

QUILLA *[KEE-lah]*
Peru

Mama Quilla, the moon who brightens the night with her silver light, was chased by a supernatural jaguar that nearly swallowed her whole twice a year. As the sky darkened during these eclipses, her worshipers gathered together, hitting rocks against each other, hollering and screeching to chase the jaguar away. Mama Quilla inspired mortals to create a calendar based on her movement through the sky.

QUINOA-MAMA *[KEEN-ah-wah MAH-mah]*
Peru

Quinoa-Mama was invoked by Peruvians each planting season, for quinoa was one of the most important grain crops used for food and in the making of beer. Women and girls made doll-size models of Quinoa-Mama from the leaves of the plant. They kept the dolls for a year before burning them in a ritual to ensure a good harvest for the next season.

RAN *[RAHN]*
Scandinavia

Ran, a mighty sea goddess, cast her huge nets through the depths of the sea, hoping to fill them with drowned sailors. Those who were lucky enough to be caught in Ran's nets were transported to her heavenly realm where they enjoyed an afterlife of pleasure and ease. Because Scandinavian sailors knew Ran was partial to gold, they often tucked a gold coin into their pockets in case a storm washed them overboard. Ran's gigantic daughters, the ocean waves, often appeared to sailors as mermaids, just like their mother.

RAUNI *[ROW-nih]*
Finland

Rauni, goddess of thunder, mated with Ukko, god of thunder, and the heavens crashed and roared for days. All the animals hid, covering their ears until the great cacophony subsided. When the sun began to shine, the animals emerged to discover tiny shoots of flowers and the stems of small trees beginning to sprout all over Earth's surface. Eventually Rauni transformed herself into the rowan tree, which is still known for its protective ability. Rowan berries are sacred to Rauni.

RHIANNON *[REE-an-non]*
Wales

Rhiannon, beautiful goddess of the moon, magic and death, was often seen riding through the forest on a glorious white horse with three singing birds perched on her shoulders. When the dead heard the birds' magical song, they were brought back to life. When the living heard it, they fell into a seven-year, deathlike sleep. In one story, a king pursued Rhiannon on horseback for three days. No matter how fast he rode, the king was unable to catch Rhiannon on her magical steed.

S

SARASVATI *[sah-RAHS-vah-tee]*
India / Hindu, Buddhist

Sarasvati, goddess of knowledge, is a gentle and graceful young woman who rides on the back of a peacock or swan, her sacred birds. She invented speech, the alphabet, poetry, literature, math and the complex patterns in Indian music. The Indian people still worship Sarasvati in libraries with offerings of fruit, flowers and incense. No reading is allowed on her sacred holiday; nor is music allowed to be played.

SEDNA *[SED-nah]*
Arctic / Inuit

Sedna, goddess of the sea, is still honored by the Inuit people. She controls the ecological balance and food supply of the Arctic Ocean. When men take too many fish or kill young animals, Sedna calls the sea creatures to her side, not allowing them to be caught. In order for fishermen to regain her favor, a shaman must journey to Sedna's huge stone house on the floor of the sea to untangle her hair. If she is pleased with his handiwork, the shaman returns to Earth's surface, the fishermen are forgiven, and Sedna once again allows humans to hunt successfully in her waters.

SEKHMET *[SEK-met]*
Egypt

Sekhmet, goddess of war and death, ruled over the scorching desert sun. Ancient Egyptians honored her ferocious power by portraying her with a lion's head. Once, when Sekhmet was offended by humans, she set about destroying all of humanity with her intense heat. She was later placed on the brow of Ra, Egypt's supreme sun god, to protect him from his enemies. Because she was also protectress of the embalmed dead, mortals placed statues of Sekhmet in the form of a woman with a lioness head at the entrance of tombs.

SHEKINAH *[shuh-KEE-nah]*
Mesopotamia / Canaan

Shekinah is described in Hebrew lore as the mother of the mysterious spirit world. She is the feminine part of all that exists. Sometimes Shekinah is described as a door or gateway, a house or a sacred shrine. Sometimes she is portrayed as the tree of life that feeds all beings. Girls and women continue to invoke Shekinah for guidance and wisdom, and for her blessings.

TARA *[TAH-rah]*
Tibet and India / Hindu, Jain and Buddhist

Tara, goddess of self-mastery, was the first woman to become what is known as a buddha or enlightened one. She devoted her mortal life to gaining enlightenment and spiritual wisdom. Even today, compassionate Tara helps mortals who worship her to overcome their fear. She appears in twenty-one forms, offering assistance with twenty-one different aspects of life. As White Tara, she is the calm, meditative goddess who gives serenity to her worshipers. As Green Tara, her fierceness tears away false beliefs. She also appears with red, yellow and blue skin, each representing a different power. Tara answers the prayers of all who call her name.

TIAMAT *[tee-YAH-maht]*
Mesopotamia, Babylonia

Tiamat, mother of the gods, was the vast, flowing waters of the great seas in the beginning of time. Eventually, she gave birth to a rowdy, wild group of gods. When she tried to quiet her noisy, unruly children, they rebelled. Her son, Marduk hurled himself at Tiamat in the form of a roaring hurricane and killed her, splitting her in two. Recognizing his mother's enormous creativity, Marduk took one part of her body and made the sky.
With the other part, he created Earth.

THEMIS *[THEM-is]*
Greece

Themis, goddess of law and order, was invoked at the beginning of every ceremony in the ancient Greek world. With her blessing, a meeting would proceed in an orderly, productive fashion. Without it, there would be chaos and no resolution. After the flood that destroyed the world, Themis gave the order to repopulate the planet.

TLAZOLTEOTL *[tlah-sohl-TAY-otl]*
Mexico / Aztec

Tlazolteotl, goddess of witchcraft, used her broom to cleanse the Aztec world of evil, theft, gambling and dishonesty, which some stories say she created! When people make confessions to Tlazolteotl, she washes her hands in a mixture of green and yellow water. Although she has the power to forgive the worst sins, she can only do this once in each person's lifetime. Tlazolteotl haunts crossroads and plagues people with temptation when they are making difficult decisions.

U

UA-ZIT *[WAHD-zet or WAHD-jet]*

Egypt

Ua-Zit, the cobra goddess, is one of the oldest known goddesses.
The ancient Egyptians believed she was the watchful eye of the universe,
rising over the heads of queens and kings for thousands of years in the form
of a cobra, her hood fully open, ready to strike. Ua-Zit was known as a
nourishing and fierce, protective mother.

UKE-MOCHI *[u-KEE-moh-chee]*

Japan / Shinto

Uke-Mochi, goddess of food, blessed the Earth with abundance. When she
opened her mouth, mounds of boiled rice spewed forth. When she turned
toward the sea, fish poured forth, and when she turned toward the mountains,
wild game rushed out of her mouth. Millet grew out of her forehead. And from
other parts of her body, wheat and beans appeared. Her eyebrows turned into
silk worms, which were immediately taken to Ama-terasu, goddess of the sun,
who then founded the art of weaving with silk. And finally, Uke-Mochi's
head grew into a cow and a horse.

UMA *[OO-mah]*
India / Hindu

Golden-skinned Uma is worshiped as the first hazy light of dawn and the soft rosy light of dusk. The Hindu people describe her as a mountain ghost who haunts the Himalayas as wisps of barely visible mist. She is also called Gracious One, for she inspires kindness and grace in mortals.

URD *[URD]*
Scandinavia

Urd was the eldest of the three sisters known as the Norns, the goddesses of destiny. Together, they watered the Tree of Life each morning with water from Urd's sacred well. While the gods gathered beside the well to hold their court of justice, the Norns sat within their home beneath the gigantic roots of the tree, crafting the story of each mortal's life from the moment of birth to the moment of death.

V

VACH *[VAHK]*
India / Hindu

Vach governs sound, the source of speech and language. Because Vach knows the secrets and power of both written and spoken communication, the Indian people consider her a goddess of wisdom. Sometimes Vach takes the form of a cow, nourishing humans with strength and energy. In this form, she is known as Melodious Cow.

VANDYA *[VAND-yah]*
India / Hindu

Vandya, goddess of the first blossoms, emerges from the sacred tree in the center of each Indian village. Every spring, as she pulls her tall, translucent self through the bark of the tree, she walks a short distance, turns and assesses how much the tree has grown. Then, Vandya runs toward the tree with a loving intention and gently kicks its trunk to wake it up and open the tree's blossoms. Vandya is one of the Yakshini, a group of goddesses who live within sacred trees.

VESTA   *[VES-tah]*
Italy

Vesta, goddess of the hearth, was worshiped several times a day in the homes of Romans as they gathered at mealtimes. The fireplace was central to every Roman home, which made Vesta one of the primary goddesses in people's lives. A group of young priestesses, known as the Vestal Virgins, tended the eternal flame in Vesta's temple. Every year on March 1st, they put out the flame, thoroughly cleaned the temple, and relit the fire by rubbing two sticks of wood together. Vesta is similar to the Greek goddess Hestia.

VIRGIN OF GUADALUPE   *[gooah-dah-LOO-peh]*
Mexico / Aztec

The Virgin of Guadalupe, goddess of mercy and compassion, nurtures and protects the Mexican people. She first appeared to a peasant in 1531, asking him to build a shrine in her honor. When the local bishop refused to believe the peasant, the Virgin gave him a cloak full of roses to take to the bishop. The bishop opened the cloak, and the roses miraculously turned into a painting of an Indian woman adorned in a garment of stars, standing on a crescent moon. A shrine was built on the spot where the Virgin had first appeared, which is now a great cathedral visited every year by thousands of pilgrims. The Virgin of Guadalupe is the patron saint of Mexico. She is celebrated on December 9th.

W

WAWALAG SISTERS *[WAH-wah-lahg]*
Australia / Aborigine

The Wawalag Sisters are fertility goddesses who journeyed across the land, blessing Earth with plants and gardens in the time before time. Toward the end of their journey, they set up a camp next to a waterhole, unaware that a great rainbow serpent goddess named Julunggul lived in the pond. Not knowing that it was forbidden to bathe there, they did so, and Julunggul immediately leaped out of the water, calling for flooding rains to cleanse the pond and to drown the Wawalag Sisters. The sisters struggled to hypnotize the great serpent, but they finally fell to the ground exhausted. As they slept, Julunggul swallowed them whole, and later spit them out, still whole — repeating this several times. Each place where the serpent regurgitated the Wawalag Sisters became a sacred place.

WHITE BUFFALO WOMAN
North America / Lakota Brule Sioux

White Buffalo Woman is a teacher of sacred ceremony who appeared to the Lakota people in a cloud of swirling dust. She showed them how to use the pipe as a form of prayer, and she reminded them to honor Earth and all animals and children as part of one family. She explained the passage of the four ages of time by turning herself into several different colored buffalos, finally disappearing in the form of a white buffalo. The Lakota still remember her in their ceremonies as a great spiritual teacher.

WILD PONY
North America / Apache

Wild Pony is honored by the Apache people as the first woman on Earth. A spirit-being told Wild Pony how to shape clay into a bowl and how to fire it so it would hold water. Many years later, when she was an old woman, Wild Pony was instructed in a dream to teach young girls how to make these bowls as well as the sacred pipe that is used in ceremonies to honor the Earth.

WURIUPRANILI *[WUR-yuh-pran-ih-lee]*
Australia / Aborigine

Wuriupranili, goddess of the sun, lit a torch of bark each morning and carried it across the sky from east to west. At the end of the day, she dipped her torch into the sea to extinguish it. The bright red color of dawn and dusk are said to come from the red powder she placed on her body. During the night, Wuriupranili journeyed through the underworld to get back to her starting place by the next morning.

X

XI WANG MU   *[SHEE WANG MU]*
China / Taoist

Xi Wang Mu, who created all living things in the universe, looks over women, protecting and guiding them throughout their lives. She is often portrayed as a woman with a leopard tail and the teeth of a tiger or dog. Xi Wang Mu lives in a palace of jade in the far west mountains where she grows peaches of immortality in her garden. Every 3,000 years, her peach trees ripen, providing fruit for the gods and goddesses. A blue stork, an albino tiger, a deer and a huge tortoise are her sacred animals.

XOCHIQUETZAL   *[show-chee-KET-zahl]*
Mexico / Aztec

Xochiquetzal, goddess of the dead, was a beautiful young maiden who taught the arts of weaving, spinning, painting and carving, as well as playing drums and pipes. The marigold, her sacred flower, is a symbol of the cycle of life for Mexicans — the opening bud, the blossoming flower, and the withering flower turning to seed for the next generation. On the Day of the Dead, Xochiquetzal's worshipers still place huge piles of marigolds at the feet of Xochiquetzal's statues. Xochiquetzal brings good luck to children.

X

YEMOJA *[yay-moh-jah]*
Nigeria / Yoruba and Central America, Haiti and Cuba

Yemoja is the mother of all waters on Earth. As a river goddess, she flows forcefully into the sea where she looks over and protects fishermen. As a goddess of fresh springs, she rolls over in her sleep and water gushes out of her round body. Yemoja is known as Yemaya in Central America, where she rules over pregnancy, childbirth and all things that concern women.

YOLKAI ESTSAN *[yol-kye es-TAHN]*
North America / Navajo

Yolkai Estsan, goddess of the moon, created the first people — making the first woman from yellow corn and the first man from white corn. She, herself, was born in a cradle of rainbows at dawn. Just before a great flood washed her away to the white sands of the desert, the Great Spirit ordered her to enter an abalone shell. When the waters subsided, Yolkai Estsan created fire, ruling over the dawn and the sea.

Z

ZARAMAMA *[ZAR-rah-MAH-mah]*
Peru

Zaramama is a grain mother who rules over corn. Some stories say she lives in the corn stalk itself. When corn was planted, Peruvian girls and women constructed and decorated corn dolls with miniature clothing and jewels as part of Zaramama's festivals. The women then tied the dolls to the branches of willow trees, and dancers encircled the trees as they prayed to Zaramama for a bountiful crop.

ZOE [ZOH-ee]
Near East / Gnostic

Zoe is one of the angels who breathed life into the first human. After many gods tried and failed, Zoe succeeded in giving life to the first man on Earth. Angered by Zoe's success, the god of creation insulted Zoe, whose strength surprised him as she threw him into a bottomless pit.

THE ZORYA [ZOR-yah]
Czechoslovakia

The three Zorya were ancient goddesses of destiny, known as She of the Evening, She of Midnight, and She of the Morning. Together, they guarded the wolf of doom, who was chained to the constellation the Little Bear so that he would not get loose and bring on the end of the world.

Goddesses by Country / Culture / Domain

AFRICA

Egypt
BASTET — Sun, healing
HATHOR — Gentle Cow, light, the sycamore tree
ISIS — Healing, corn, handicrafts
QADESH — Love, fertility
SEKHMET — Fire, desert heat, sun
UA-ZIT — Magic, wisdom, regeneration

Nigeria
OBA — Water, rivers
OSHUN — Mother of the first people, protects women leaders
YEMOJA — Mother of all waters

South Africa
MBABA MWANA WARESA — Rain clouds, lightning, thunder

Togo
NGOLIMENTO — Mother of spirits, protects unborn children

ASIA

China
CHANG-E — Moon, protects sleeping children
ETERNA — Magic
FENG-PO — Old Woman of the Wind
KUAN YIN — She Who Hears the Cries of the World, compassion
NÜ WA — Marriage, creation
XI WANG MU — Immortality, women

India
ADITI — Creatrix, Mother of the Universe
DURGA — Warrior
KALI — Life and death, warrior
LAKSHMI — Prosperity, beauty, pleasure, success
SARASVATI — Knowledge, speech, language, literature
TARA — Self-mastery, enlightenment
UMA — Dawn and dusk, love
VACH — Sound, wisdom
VANDYA — Adorableness, makes the trees blossom

Japan
AMA-TERASU — Sun
BENTEN — Good luck, sea
KAGUYA-HIME — Moon
KO-NO-HANA — She Who Makes the Flowers of the Trees Open, beauty
UKE-MOCHI — Food, rice, fish, beans

EUROPE

Albania
THE FATIT — Fate

Czechoslovakia
ZORYA — Dawn, dusk and midnight

France
EPONA — Horses
KORRIGAN — Underground springs, protectress of women

Germany
OSTARA — Spring, abundance

Greece & Crete
APHRODITE — Love and beauty
ARTEMIS — Lady of the Beast, protectress of girls
ATHENA — Wisdom, invention
BRITOMARTIS — Moon, blesses fishermen, hunters, sailors
CYBELE — Mountains and caves, mother of the gods
DEMETER — Vegetation
ECHO — Mountain nymph
EIRENE — Peace, one of the Horae
EURYNOME — Great Wandering One, creatrix
GAIA — Earth, Mother of All
THE GRACES — Kindness, good manners
THE GRAEAE — Sea, sisters of the Gorgons
HEKATE — Night, moon, magic
HERA — Women, childbirth, leadership
HESTIA — Domestic harmony
IRIS — Rainbow, messenger of Hera
MEDUSA — Sea, transformation
THE MUSES — Arts and sciences
NIKE — Victory
PANDORA — All-giving, abundance
PERSEPHONE — Queen of the dead, spring
THEMIS — Law and order

Ireland
BABD — War goddess
BRIGIT — Fire, healing, poetry, crafts
CAILLEACH BEARA — Seasons, agriculture, lakes

MACHA — Earth, the land, war, prophesy

Italy
EPONA — Horses
FORTUNA — Luck and chance, fertility
JUNO — Goddess of women, pregnancy, birth, family harmony
OPS — Abundance, fertility
VESTA — Goddess of fire, hearth

Scandinavia
BEIWE — Sun, spring, fertility
ELLI — Old age and death
FREYA — Desire, love, war and death
HEL — Death, guide to the dead
IDUNA — Youth and strength, invented the runes
RAN — Sea
RAUNI — Thunder
URD — Destiny, one of the Norns

Wales
OLWEN — Sun, White Lady of the Day
RHIANNON — Enchantment

NEAR EAST

HANNA HANNA — Grandmother of All, wisdom, destiny
INANNA — War and love, Queen of Heaven
LILITH — Night, independence, newborn babies
NINLIL — Moon, winds
SHEKINAH — Wisdom, She Who Dwells Within
TIAMAT — Sea, mother of the gods
ZOE — Life-giver

NORTH AMERICA

Apache
WILD PONY — First woman, teacher of ceremony to young girls

Inuit
SEDNA — Sea, protects the animals of the sea

Iroquois
AATAENTSIC — Creation
GENDENWITHA — She Who Brings the Day,
the morning star

Lakota Brule Sioux
WHITE BUFFALO WOMAN — Sacred ceremony

Navajo
ESTSANATLEHI — Time, magic, life, death and immortality

YOLKAI ESTSAN — Moon, White Shell Woman,
mother of the first people

Wintun
NORWAN — Dancing Porcupine Woman, sunlight, agriculture

OCEANIA

Australia

Aborigine
WAWALAG SISTERS — Fertility, languages
WURIUPRANILI — Sun

Goanna
LIA — Water, guardian of women

Yulengor
JUNKGOWA SISTERS — Food, waterholes

New Guinea
GOGA — Fire, sacred ceremony

New Zealand

Maori
PAPATUANUKU — Mother Earth

POLYNESIA

Hawaii
PELE — Volcanic fire, anger

SOUTH & CENTRAL AMERICA

Mexico

Aztec
CHALCHIUHTLICUE — Water of all kinds
TLAZOLTEOTL — Evil, theft, sin, Eater of Filth
VIRGIN OF GUADALUPE — Mercy and compassion
XOCHIQUETZAL — Ruler of the land of the dead, flowers,
good luck to children

Maya, Putun
IX CHEL — Moon, childbirth

Peru
MAMA PACCHA — Earth mother, bounty,
mountains, earthquakes
QUILLA — Moon, calendar, marriage
QUINOA-MAMA — Grain, fertility
ZARAMAMA — Corn

 Sources

Aldington, R. and Delano Ames, tr. *New Larousse Encyclopedia of Mythology*. Prometheus Press. The Hamlyn Publishing Group. London. 1959.

Allen, Paula Gunn. *Grandmothers of the Light*. Beacon Press. Boston. 1991.

Ardinger, Barbara. *Goddess Meditations*. Llewellyn Publications. St Paul, Minnesota. 1998.

Austen, Hallie Iglehart. *The Heart of the Goddess*. Wingbow Press. Berkeley. 1990.

Badejo, Diedre. *Osun Seegesi: The Elegant Deity of Wealth, Power and Femininity*. Africa World Press. Trenton, New Jersey. 1996.

Bell, Robert. E. *Women of Classical Mythology*. Oxford University Press. New York. 1991.

Blair, Nancy. *Goddesses for Every Season*. Element Books. Rockport, MA. 1995.

Boer, Charles, tr. *The Homeric Hymns*. Spring Publications. Dallas, Texas. 1991.

Bonnefoy, Yves. *Mythologies*. University of Chicago Press. Chicago and London. 1991.

Burkert, Walter. (John Raffan, tr.) *Greek Religion*. Harvard University Press. Cambridge, MA. 1985.

Burland, C. A. *The Gods of Mexico*. G. P. Putnam's Sons. New York. 1967.

Carlyon, Richard. *A Guide to the Gods*. William Morrow. New York. 1981.

Chicago, Judy. *The Dinner Party*. Anchor Books. Garden City, New York. 1979.

Condren, Mary. *The Serpent and the Goddess*. Harper & Row Publishers. San Francisco. 1989.

Davidson, H. R. Ellis. *Scandinavian Mythology*. Peter Bedrick Books. New York. 1969.

Downing, Christine. *The Goddess: Mythological Images of the Feminine*. Crossroad. New York. 1989.

Durdin-Robertson, Lawrence. *The Goddesses of India, Tibet, China and Japan*. Cesara Publications. Eire. 1976.

Eliade, Mircea. *Australian Religions*. Cornell University Press. Ithaca and London. 1973.

Forty, Jo. *Mythology: A Visual Encyclopedia*. PRC Publishing. London. 1999.

Garrett, John. *A Classical Dictionary of India*. Oriental Publishers. Delhi. 1871.

George, Demetra. *Mysteries of the Dark Moon*. Harper. San Francisco. 1992.

Gleason, Judith. *Oya: In Praise of the Goddess*. Shambhala Publications. Boston and London. 1987.

Gottlieb, Lynn. *She Who Dwells Within*. Harper. San Francisco. 1995.

Graves, Robert. *The Greek Myths*. Penguin Books. London. 1960.

Green, Miranda. *Celtic Goddesses — Warriors, Virgins, and Mothers*. British Museum Press. London. 1995.

Imel, Dorothy Myers and Martha Ann. *Goddesses in World Mythology*. ABC-CLIO. Santa Barbara, CA. 1993.

Ions, Veronica. *Egyptian Mythology*. The Hamlyn Publishing Group. London, New York, Sydney, Toronto. 1965.

Ions, Veronica. *Indian Mythology*. The Hamlyn Publishing Group. London, New York, Sydney, Toronto. 1973.

Jordan, Michael. *Encyclopedia of Gods*. Facts On File 1993.

Katz, Brian. *Deities and Demons of the Far East*. Metro Books. New York. 1995.

Kinsley, David. *The Goddesses' Mirror*. State University of New York Press. Albany, New York. 1989.

Leeming, David and Page, Jake. *Goddess — Myths of the Female Divine*. Oxford University Press. Oxford, New York, Toronto. 1995.

Milne, Courtney and Miller, Sherrill. *Visions of the Goddess*. Penguin Studio. Penguin Books. Toronto and New York. 1998.

Monaghan, Patricia. *O Mother Sun!* The Crossing Press. Freedom, CA. 1994.

Monaghan, Patricia. *The New Book of Goddesses and Heroines*. Llewellyn Publications. St Paul, Minnesota. 1997.

Neumann, Erich. *The Great Mother*. Princeton University Press. Princeton, New Jersey. 1963.

Oda, Mayumi. *Goddesses*. Volcano Press. Volcano, California. 1981.

Poignant, Roslyn. *Oceanic Mythology*. Paul Hamlyn. London, New York, Sydney, Toronto. 1967.

Spretnak, Charlene. *Lost Goddesses of Ancient Greece*. Beacon Press. Boston. 1978.

Stone, Merlin. *Ancient Mirrors of Womanhood*. Beacon Press. Boston. 1979.

Swain, Tony and Trompf, Carry. *The Religions of Oceania*. Routledge. New York. 1995.

Teish, Luisah. *Jambalaya*. Harper San Francisco. 1985.

Walker, Barbara. *The Woman's Dictionary of Symbols and Sacred Objects*. Harper & Row Publishers. San Francisco. 1988.

Walker, Barbara. *The Woman's Encyclopedia of Myths and Secrets*. Harper & Row Publishers. San Francisco. 1983.

Wasson, R. Gordon, Hofmann, Albert, Ruck, Carl. *The Road to Eleusis*. Harcourt Brace Jovanovich. New York and London. 1978.

Wolkstein, Diane and Kramer, Samuel. *Inanna, Queen of Heaven and Earth*. Harper & Row Publishers. New York. 1983.